THE MOST WONDERFUL DOLL
IN THE WORLD

THE MOST WONDERFUL DOLL IN THE WORLD

BY

Phyllis McGinley

WITH DRAWINGS BY

Helen Stone

SCHOLASTIC
HARDCOVER

SCHOLASTIC INC. / New York

Library of Congress Cataloging-in-Publication Data

McGinley, Phyllis, 1905- 1978
  The most wonderful doll in the world / by Phyllis McGinley ; with drawings by Helen Stone.
    p. cm.
    Summary: the memory of the doll Dulcy lost becomes more wonderful and exaggerated each time she talks about it.
    ISBN 0-590-43476-4
    [1. Dolls—Fiction.] I. Stone, Helen, 1903-   ill. II. Title.
PZ7.M1677Mob 1990
    [E]—dc20   89-70223
                                                                         CIP
                                                                         AC

12 11 10 9 8 7 6 5 4 3 2 1   0 1 2 3 4 5/9
Printed in the U.S.A.   36
First Scholastic printing, September 1990

There was once a little girl named

Dulcy

who found it hard to be satisfied with

Things as They Are

She was always wishing her fly-away hair could be ringlets or that she lived on a farm instead of in a pretty village or that she were tall and slim instead of plump and rosy-round.

"Too much imagination," her mother used to say to her father. "She'll get over it." But sometimes even they were made unhappy when Dulcy wished out loud for something bigger or better or more expensive than what she had.

Take dolls, for instance. Dulcy was very fond of dolls. And since her mother and her father and her uncles and aunts and cousins and friends were very fond of *Dulcy*, they were forever buying dolls to add to her collection. By the time she was six-going-on-seven, she had such a family of them as any other child would have been proud to own.

There were the blue-eyed twins, Jack and Jill, with a crib and a bathinette to themselves.

There was a big brown-eyed baby named Tosca, in a white christening coat. There was Miss Abernathy, her special favorite, who wore a plaid jacket and skirt. There was a little girl doll with braids, named Mary-Alicia; there was Topsy, the clown; and the ballet dancer, a dainty creature called simply Ballerina. There were little dolls and big dolls, and jointed dolls for the doll house, and a bride doll with a lace veil, and dolls who were never undressed but who merely stood on a shelf and looked charming.

Dulcy liked them all and was quite a good mother to them, taking them out for airings and giving them medicine when they fell ill. But she was always wishing Mary Alicia's hair were yellow instead of brown or that Tosca owned a lace slip like the doll of her best friend, Margery. She was always dreaming that any gift she received was just a tiny bit different or a trifle better than it was.

Tosca

Jack

Jill

Ballerina

Topsy

Miss Abernathy

Mary Alicia

The Bride

Then one day Angela came into her life. It happened like this:

On a blue, smoky afternoon in October, Dulcy was walking down the street on her way home from school. As she passed the home of Mrs. Primrose, that lady herself came to the door. Dulcy was glad to see her, for Mrs. Primrose was her particular friend. She was quite old and all her children had grown up and gone away. But she lived in a house full of things exciting to look at and to listen to. She had a music box that played twelve tunes. She had shelves full of lead soldiers. She had a canary in a cage and a paper-weight inside of which was a tiny church, standing in the snow. When you shook the paper-weight, snow fell thickly about the church from the sky.

"Dulcy," called her friend, "come here a minute. I have a present for you."

In the house, Dulcy saw that the furniture

was covered with sheets and that the canary was no longer in his cage.

"I am going away for the winter," said Mrs. Primrose. "While I was packing my things, I came across this." And, taking a doll from the mantelpiece, she put it into Dulcy's arms. Then, also from the mantel, she took a box tied with gold string and gave that to Dulcy, too.

"This doll's name is Angela," Mrs. Primrose said, "and she belonged to a child who once lived here. Now I want you to have her. In the box is her wardrobe."

"Oh, thank you," cried Dulcy. "Thank you very much, Mrs. Primrose." And she remembered to add politely, "I'm sorry you are going away."

"I'll be back," said Mrs. Primrose. "Now shake the paper-weight and run along with Angela."

So Dulcy shook the snow into a blizzard

about the church. Then she kissed Mrs.
Primrose goodbye and hurried home with
her gift. On her way she stopped several
times to peek at the clothes in the box.

"Angela's nice," she thought. But, being
Dulcy, she said to herself, "Only I wish she
had black hair instead of yellow. Margery's
new doll has hair as black as coal."

Still, she skipped along happily until she
reached the path that led to her own house.
Then she saw that something exciting was

going on. It was leaf-raking time and the gardener had gathered up all the leaves from under the trees and around the hedges and upon the lawn and was preparing to set them afire.

"A bonfire!" cried Dulcy. And propping Angela carelessly against one of the leaf-piles which had not yet been gathered into the center mound, she hurried off to watch the flames. All afternoon she helped to burn those leaves and to rake scattered heaps of them into the blaze. It was only when her mother called her to come in to wash her hands for supper that Dulcy suddenly remembered about Angela.

But when she ran to the spot where she was sure the doll was sitting, no Angela was to be found. Nor was the box anywhere in sight.

Dulcy searched and searched. Her mother came out to help her. Even though the gardener said he was certain that Angela must have been raked into the bonfire, he joined in the hunt too, until it was too dark to look any longer. They had finally to admit that Angela had disappeared.

Poor Dulcy! Although there was chicken and ice cream for supper, she could scarcely eat a bite. Now that Angela was lost, she realized what a treasure it was that Mrs. Primrose had given her.

"Tell me about Angela," said Dulcy's mother, trying to console her. "Perhaps we can find a doll almost like her."

"She was beautiful," sobbed Dulcy. "She had yellow hair and eyes that opened and closed and a blue dress with a pinafore."

"Dolls with yellow hair and eyes that open and close and blue dresses with pinafores shouldn't be too hard to find," Dulcy's mother said. "When I'm down town I'll buy you another."

"There'll never be another Angela," cried Dulcy. Across her mind floated a picture of the doll as she would have looked in one of those costumes from the box tied with gold string. Surely Angela would have been finer than any doll she owned. "She wore patent leather shoes. Real patent leather shoes with *heels*. And she could say Mama and Papa and sing Rockabye Baby."

"Why, what a remarkable doll she must have been," exclaimed Dulcy's mother. "I doubt if I could find another like *that*."

"I lost my doll," Dulcy told her father when he came home late from the office. "Her name was Angela and she had yellow hair and eyes that opened and closed and she wore patent leather shoes with *heels*. And she could say Mama and Papa and sing Rockabye Baby."

"Never mind, Dulcy," said her father. "I'll get you a doll to take her place."

"Oh, no," mourned Dulcy, who had been thinking and thinking about the splendors the bonfire had taken from her. "There'll never be another Angela. She was the most

wonderful doll in the world. She could sing
Rockabye Baby and wave her hand and take
steps."

"Oh, goodness gracious!" said Dulcy's father. "She must have been one of those old clockwork dolls. I don't think they are made any longer."

And, sure enough, although he looked in all the shops the next afternoon, he couldn't find a doll like Angela.

Every day when Dulcy came home from school, she searched beneath the hedges and under the trees, hoping that Angela had somehow been overlooked. But fresh leaves kept floating down from the maples and covering up the raked lawn, and then the rains came, and then the snow, and Angela was finally given up for good. But the more Dulcy thought about her, the more marvels she remembered.

"Did you know I had lost my doll?" she asked her teacher at school.

"No, Dulcy," answered her teacher. "I

hadn't heard. Tell me about her."

"She was the most wonderful doll in the world," Dulcy said eagerly. "Her name was Angela and she had real yellow hair and eyes that opened and closed and she said Mama and Papa and sang Rockabye Baby. She wore patent leather shoes with *heels* and she could wave her hand. And take steps."

"Maybe you'll find one like her," said the teacher.

"There'll never be another Angela," Dulcy sighed. She closed her own eyes a moment and thought about it. "She had a purse with a handkerchief in it and little tiny leather gloves."

"Dear me," remarked the teacher. "What an unusual doll she must have been!"

Dulcy said, sadly, "Yes, she was." And when she got home that night she looked at her doll family with great dissatisfaction, indeed.

"Angela was so much nicer than you," she said to Miss Abernathy, crossly. And taking her out of the chair, she shut her away in a cupboard drawer.

Aunt Tabitha came to visit Dulcy's parents soon after that. Aunt Tabby was nearly Dulcy's favorite relative. She was young and gay and knew many interesting stories, and she always carried a present in her traveling bag for Dulcy. This time the present turned out to be a doll, and a pretty one, dressed like a skater. But Dulcy burst into tears when Aunt Tabby handed it to her.

"Whatever is the matter with the child?" cried Aunt Tabby.

"I had a doll named Angela and I lost her," wept Dulcy. "And she was the most wonderful doll in the world. She had real yellow hair and eyes that opened and closed and she could say Mama and Papa and sing Rockabye Baby. And she wore patent leather shoes with *heels* and she could wave her hand. And take steps. She had a purse with a handkerchief in it and little tiny leather gloves."

"But look—this doll has a skating costume," Aunt Tabby coaxed.

Dulcy stopped and thought about that for a time. "So did Angela," she cried. "And she had skates, too, that you could take off and put on. And when you wound her up,

she skated!

"Oh dear me," said Aunt Tabitha. "I don't know where you would ever find another doll like that. You'll just have to get along with this one."

So Dulcy thanked her but when she went upstairs she put the Skater in the drawer along with Miss Abernathy, and after a minute she picked up Mary Alicia and put her in the cupboard, also.

When Margery came over to play, Dulcy suggested that they have a game of hide-and-seek instead of dressing up like nurses and playing doll hospital.

"Since I lost Angela, I don't feel like waiting on the others," she told Margery.

"Who was Angela?" asked her friend.

"She was the most wonderful doll in the world," said Dulcy. "She had real yellow hair and eyes that opened and closed and patent leather shoes with *heels* and a purse with a handkerchief in it and little tiny leather

gloves. She could say Mama and Papa and sing Rockabye Baby and wave her hand and take steps. She had skates you could put on and take off and when you wound her up she *skated*."

"Won't your parents give you another?" Margery wanted to know.

"There'll never be another Angela," said Dulcy. "She had a raincoat, too. And rubbers. And a teentsy umbrella that you could put up when it rained."

So they played hide-and-seek and parchesi instead of hospital. And that night before she went to bed, Dulcy looked scornfully at her dolls and shut the Twins away in the cupboard with Miss Abernathy and Mary Alicia and the Skater.

The news of the lost doll spread about the school.

At recess all the little girls begged Dulcy to describe her.

"She was the most wonderful doll in the world," Dulcy told them, sorrowfully. "Her name was Angela and she had real yellow hair and eyes that opened and closed and patent leather shoes with *heels* and a purse with a handkerchief in it and little tiny gloves and skates that you could put on and take off. When you wound her up she *skated*. And she could wave her hand and take steps. And she had a raincoat and rubbers and a teentsy umbrella that you could put up when it rained."

"My doll has a nightgown and a bathrobe," said one of the little girls.

Dulcy remembered hard.

"So had Angela," she declared. "She had a nightgown and bathrobe to match. And pajamas and red velvet slippers that turned up at the toes."

"I guess she didn't have a riding costume like my doll," said one of the third graders who was listening.

"Of *course*, she did," said Dulcy. "She had a riding costume and she had a little bathing suit with a rubber cap."

"Oh, goodness!" said the little girls. "You'll never find another doll like that!"

"No, I won't," Dulcy said. And that night she put the Ballerina in the cupboard along with Miss Abernathy and Mary Alicia and the Skater and the Twins.

"Did you hear about Angela?" Dulcy asked her grandmother when her grandmother came to spend the day. "I've lost her and she was the most wonderful doll in the world. She had real yellow hair and eyes that opened and closed and patent leather shoes with *heels* and a purse with a handkerchief in it and little tiny gloves and skates that you could put on and take off. When you wound her up she *skated*. She could say Mama and Papa and sing Rockabye Baby and wave her hand and take steps. And she had a raincoat and rubbers and a teentsy umbrella that you could put up when it rained. And a nightgown and a bathrobe to match and pajamas and red velvet slippers that turned up at the toes. And a riding costume and a little bathing suit with a rubber cap."

"Well, now," said Dulcy's grandmother. "I'll get you another doll when I go to the city. I saw one the other day—a doll with a cowgirl suit like yours."

"Angela had a cowgirl suit, too," said

Dulcy proudly. "And a tiny gun in a tiny holster. And spurs."

"Oh, dear," said Dulcy's grandmother. "I expect I'll have to get you something else then." So when she went to the city, she sent Dulcy a box of water colors which Dulcy had to give away because she already owned a set exactly like them. And it made Dulcy so dissatisfied that she took the bride doll and shut her away in the drawer to keep company with Miss Abernathy, Mary Alicia, the Twins, the Skater, and the Ballerina.

By the time the winter was over, only the doll-house dolls remained in their proper

places. And that was because Dulcy scarcely
ever played with them. No one dared to give

her dolls any longer because none of them
could measure up to Angela. Her father

stopped bringing dolls home with him on special occasions like Valentine's Day and Easter. Aunt Tabby brought her only candy —the hard kind that Dulcy disliked. On her birthday she had a birthday party but all she received were clothes and games. What is more, Dulcy's friends grew tired of having their own dolls compared to Angela. After a while they left off inviting Dulcy to their houses. Nobody wanted to hear another word about the famous lost doll.

When Marianne's mother knitted a stocking cap for Marianne's Cry-Baby, Dulcy spoke of the cap and sweater and *mittens* that had belonged to Angela. When Catherine's doll got new sheets for her bed, Dulcy remembered that Angela had come supplied with sheets and a pink satin quilt. Even Margery stopped listening and went home one day when right in the middle of a game of Monopoly, Dulcy began, "Did I ever tell you about Angela's green taffeta party dress?"

Soon Dulcy was spending her afternoons
alone. By that time it was spring and the

leaves were beginning to come out on the trees.

And it was in the spring—on a blue smoky Saturday almost like that day last fall—when Angela came back!

Dulcy had been playing hop-scotch with a new little girl named Isabel, who had moved into the second house from the corner on Dulcy's street.

When the noon whistle blew they stopped their game and sat down on a stone seat at the very end of the garden to rest a moment before their mothers called them to lunch. While they were kicking their feet in last year's leaves which had drifted under the stone, Dulcy said wistfully to Isabel,

"Did I tell you about the doll I lost?"

"No," said Isabel, who had moved into her house only the Saturday before.

"She was the most wonderful doll in the world," Dulcy began dreamily as she had so many times before. "She had real yellow hair and eyes that opened and closed and she said Mama and Papa and sang Rockabye Baby, and she could wave her hand and take steps. She had patent leather shoes with *heels* and a purse with a handkerchief in it and little tiny gloves and skates you could put on and take off. When you wound her up, she skated! She had a raincoat and rubbers and a teentsy umbrella that you could put up when it rained. And a nightgown and a bathrobe to match and pajamas and red velvet slippers that turned up at the toes. And a riding costume and a little bathing suit with a rubber cap. And a cowgirl suit. With a tiny gun in a tiny holster. And spurs. And a cap and a sweater and mittens and sheets for her bed and a pink satin quilt and a green taffeta dress for parties."

"My doll has a Sunday coat," said Isabel.
Dulcy hardly had to think at all. "So did
Angela," she said quickly. "She had a Sun-
day coat with gaiters and a tam-o-shanter.
There was a feather in the tam-o-shanter."

"I wish I could have seen her," said Isabel, kicking her feet merrily. Suddenly her heel struck something buried in the leaves. She leaned down and tugged. Whatever it was had lain for a long while unnoticed beneath the stone seat. Dulcy helped her pull, and out from the leaves came a dismal looking object, muddy and faded by the winter weather. For a moment they both stared at it.

"It looks like a doll," said Isabel. Then she leaned down and poked among the leaves again. This time she pulled out a box, dirty and tied with tarnished gold string.

"These look like doll clothes," she said, tearing away the discolored lid. "Poor old doll. She's been left out of doors for ever so long." And she began smoothing down the limp hair and brushing the mud from the frock.

Dulcy gave a squeal of surprise. "Why, it's Angela," she started to say. Then she looked once more at the forlorn little figure.

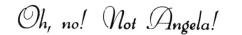

Oh, no! Not Angela!

Surely not. This doll was small and although her hair must certainly have once been yellow and her eyes could possibly open and close, she wasn't the least like the Angela she remembered.

50

"This couldn't be Angela," Isabel said. "This doll doesn't say Mama or Papa."

"No," Dulcy agreed, swallowing hard.

"And she doesn't have many clothes," Isabel went on, looking through the things in the box. "There aren't any raincoats or rubbers or bathrobes or bathing suits."

"No," said Dulcy. She looked sadly at the few simple dresses laid out before her.

"There's no cowgirl suit. I don't see any sweater or mittens or teentsy umbrella. And this doll couldn't wave her hand or skate in a million trillion years. And she doesn't have any green taffeta party dress or Sunday coat with gaiters."

"No," Dulcy gulped again.

"She doesn't even have patent leather shoes with heels," Isabel cried. "She's just an ordinary doll. I wonder where she came from." And she threw the funny, dirty little figure carelessly into Dulcy's lap. "Come on, let's play another game before lunch."

"No," said Dulcy in a strange voice. And picking up the doll, she ran fast into the house and up to her room.

It was there that her mother found her when she came to say that the sandwiches were ready. Dulcy was sitting on the bed, staring straight in front of her. On a chair sat the doll, dried off a bit and cleaner, but still rather a sorry looking sight.

"Where in the world did you get this thing?" asked Dulcy's mother. "I thought you never played with dolls any more."

Dulcy drew a deep breath. "It's—it's Angela," she said. "It's Angela! I found her. And she doesn't talk or sing or skate or wave her hand and she doesn't have shoes with heels or a purse or a raincoat or gloves or an umbrella or anything at all that's wonderful. I must have just made it all up out of my head."

"Oh, poor Dulcy!" cried her mother. She put her arms around Dulcy and held her fast. "You imagined it."

Dulcy still didn't cry.

"Yes," she said. "I imagined it." Then she let just two round tears fall from her eyes and down her cheeks. "But I thought it was true. I *did* think I remembered."

"Poor Dulcy," her mother murmured again. Then she said something strange but which Dulcy understood.

"Everybody has a dream," said Dulcy's mother. "And sometimes people get mixed up about what is dream and what is real. That's how it happened with Angela. You remembered your dream of her."

"Yes," said Dulcy, "it was the way I wanted her to be."

"But as we grow up," Dulcy's mother continued, "we learn to be more satisfied with Things as They Are."

"Don't grown-ups have dreams?" asked Dulcy.

"Oh, yes," her mother said. "Of course

they do. But they know the difference between what is true and what is not. They keep the dream glowing like a little fire at which they can warm their hearts."

"Well," said Dulcy and drew a deep breath. "I'll have to grow up, I guess." And going to the cupboard, she took out Miss Abernathy and Mary Alicia and Jack and Jill and Tosca and the Skater and the Ballerina and the rest of the family who had been so patient there through the long dark months.

"All winter," Dulcy told her mother, "I didn't have much fun because I was thinking about that imaginary Angela. Now I'll play with all my dolls. I'd forgotten how much I liked them. And I'll ask Margery back this very afternoon. I'll even let her see how the real Angela looks."

Then she stopped and thought for a moment. "But some day," said Dulcy, "maybe I'll find a doll that's something like my dream.

Only her name will be Veronica. And her party dress will be yellow instead of green and she'll have coal-black curls."

"Perhaps you will," said her mother. "Now come and have your lunch."

It wasn't long after this that Mrs. Primrose returned to the house she had left. Dulcy went to visit her. She saw the canary in the cage and played the music box and examined the lead soldiers and made a snowstorm in the paper weight.

As she was leaving, Mrs. Primrose asked her, "How is Angela?"

"Angela's fine, thank you," said Dulcy cheerfully. "I lost her for a while, then I found her again and she's one of my favorites." She paused and looked up at her friend. "But I have another doll, now, Mrs.

Primrose. Her name is Veronica and she's the most wonderful doll in the world. She has coal-black curls and eyes that open and close and she says Mama and Papa and sings Rockabye Baby and she can wave her hand and take steps. She has patent leather shoes with *heels* and a purse with a little handkerchief in it and little tiny gloves. And skates that you can take off and put on. When you wind her up, she skates. She has a rain coat and rubbers and a teentsy umbrella that you can put up when it rains; and a nightgown and bathrobe to match. And pajamas. And red velvet slippers that turn up at the toes. And a riding costume and a little bathing suit with a rubber cap. And a cowgirl suit. With a tiny gun in a tiny holster. And spurs. And a cap and a sweater and mittens and sheets for her bed and a satin quilt and a green—I mean a yellow—taffeta party dress and a Sunday coat with gaiters and a tam-o-shanter that has

61

a feather. Oh, yes, and a muff made out of real fur."

"My goodness!" cried Mrs. Primrose, astonished. "What a remarkable doll she must be. "Wherever did you get her?"

Dulcy looked solemnly at Mrs. Primrose. Her eyes opened very wide. Then all of a sudden she began to giggle. "Nowhere," she said. "I made her up out of my head. She's just imaginary. But my other dolls don't mind and I'm very fond of Veronica."

"I see," said Mrs. Primrose. "She sounds like a very fine sort of playmate." Then she, too, paused and looked Dulcy over from head

to toe. "Why child!" she exclaimed. "How tall you're getting! And I think you have changed while I've been away. Dulcy, I *do* believe you're growing up."

The End